I STARTED SCHOOL TODAY

Written and Illustrated by

Karen G. Frandsen

 CHILDRENS PRESS, CHICAGO

Library of Congress Cataloging in Publication Data

Frandsen, Karen G.
  I started school today.

   Summary: A young child reports on the first day at
school—fraught with both anxiety and pleasant surprises.
   [1. Schools—Fiction]   I.   Title.
PZ7.F8488Iaf 1984   [E]   83-23169
ISBN O-516-O3495-2

I started school today.

My mom said I was
going to learn to read.

When we got to
school, all the kids
waited outside. All
the moms watched us.

Then, the school
bell rang. All the kids
went inside and all the
moms went home.

Susie started crying.

Jason couldn't find
the bathroom.

And I just wanted
to go home to see
if any stranger
was taking my toys.

My teacher smiled
at me. She said I might
want to wait because we
were going to have
chocolate cupcakes later.

I saved part of
my cupcake for her.
I put it on her chair
to surprise her.

I like surprises.

She sat down
on her chair before
she took the cupcake
off. I think she was
surprised.

Then she smiled at me.
I like my teacher.

Later we made rules that said
    take turns
    don't hit
    raise hands
    listen
    be quiet
    don't run
    line up
    share
    whisper
    don't yell.

19

Well pretty soon it was
time to go home.

I still couldn't read,

but we all lined up
to go home anyway.

I rode on the bus.
The bus driver went
right past my house.
She stopped at the
corner instead.

Johnny said I might
as well get off with him.
He was thinking of
running away, and we
could do it together.

It's great to have a
friend like Johnny, but. . .

I was hungry and I
wanted to see if any
stranger had taken my
toys. . .

so

I

walked
home.

Maybe tomorrow
I'll learn how to read.

Tomorrow I will
take my dead lizard
to school and surprise
my teacher again.

I like my teacher.

About the author /artist

Karen Frandsen grew up in southern California and presently lives in San Diego with her children, Eric and Ingrid.

Ms. Frandsen is a free-lance artist and elementary school teacher.

The real experiences of her two children and her students are the basis for her **I Started School Today.**